FILTHY VANDAL

A JUNKYARD SHIFTERS PREQUEL

LIZA STREET

Filthy Vandal, A Junkyard Shifters Prequel

by Liza Street

Cover designed by Keira Blackwood.

Copyright 2020 Liza Street. All rights reserved.

This book is a work of fiction. Names, characters, places, and incidents either are products of the author's imagination or are used fictitiously. Any resemblance to actual persons, living or dead, events, or locales is entirely coincidental or used fictitiously.

PROLOGUE

The ceiling of Grant's porch needed another coat of paint. He didn't like buying paint if he could help it. He'd have to barter with one of the Junkyard shifters to find him some in the dump. Just as easy and a helluva lot cheaper to get an old can than to drive twenty miles into town to buy a new one.

It was warm for February. A fly buzzed past, drawing his attention to the boundary between his modest property and the Junkyard nearby. An empty camp trailer sat at the edge, an eyesore dragged there by one of the shifters inside the territory and then abandoned. Whoever had moved it must've gone to some effort getting it all the way across the Junkyard—the dump was on the far side of the ninety-acre territory. Now the door faced Grant's cabin. The plastic siding had yellowed with age and Grant itched to give it a good coat of paint, too. Or better, burn it down.

Grant reached down for his beer and the hammock swung gently. Despite the ugly as hell camp trailer nearby, this was the fuckin' life—resting easy, day in, day out. Painting in the garage when it got cold, and on warm days, hauling canvases outside and painting in the sunlight.

His phone buzzed on the porch floor beneath him, and he cursed.

This life was easy until one of the west coast alphas called him for help with a Junkyard run. Idiots. Any moron could throw a shifter into the Junkyard. You take a bad guy, you push him across the magical boundary, and bam. He's stuck forever, and the world is a safer place.

The name on his phone read *Hutchins*. He was the alpha of the Halfmoon Clan in northern Nevada. Grant picked up his phone and answered, "Yeah. Lewiston here."

"Shipment coming in," a gruff voice said.

Inwardly, Grant winced. Shipment? He knew they were bad guys, but they were still *guys*, not "shipments."

"You there?" Hutchins asked.

"Yeah. How many?"

"Two. But I gotta warn you—one isn't interested in going quietly."

"They never are." Grant sighed.

He and Hutchins worked out logistics and the call ended with Grant staring at the old trailer that sat just on the other side of a line of what looked like gravel. It wasn't merely gravel, though; it anchored a powerful spell.

The rest of the day passed in a blur of paint and canvas. Grant used the art to keep himself from thinking too hard about the job ahead. When twilight rolled around, he put away his canvases and paints, rinsed out his brushes, and stretched, trying to shake off the intense focus painting had brought on. He opened another beer and set it beside his hammock—the drink would be waiting for him when he was through with the transfer.

A vehicle's engine rumbled. Far away, still, but Grant would need to hustle to take himself all the way around the Junkyard to the road that led to the dump. The run took him through forest and his inner mountain lion reveled in the scents and sounds of nature. Snow clung to the shadows of trees and boulders, but new grasses punched up in the sunny patches on the ground.

Soon, he reached the "real" dump—the area of the Junkyard that was filled with old cars, scrap metal, and random furniture castaways. Humans didn't bring their castoffs here anymore, and it hadn't ever been used for regular household garbage, which was a plus. Otherwise, the place's smell would've been intolerable to any shifter.

A van rolled up and parked in the dirt lot next to the boundary. Grant ambled over while the driver climbed out. Young guy, scrappy, looked like he couldn't weigh more than a buck thirty. His thick, bushy eyebrows probably weighed more than the rest of him. Grant frowned. *This* was a guy some asshole had sent to transport vicious shifters who weren't fit for society?

"Are you Grant?" the kid asked.

"Yep."

"Cool. I've heard a lot about you. You throw 'em in and watch the boundary?"

"Pretty much, yeah."

The kid nodded and his giant eyebrows went up and

down in time with his nodding. "What's it like living without a pack?"

"My pride wasn't much to miss," Grant said.

"Pride...whoa, so you're a lion shifter? Wicked."

"Mountain lion. Yep." Big cats lived in prides, bears lived in clans, and wolves lived in packs.

Grant stood, waiting. The kid stared at him. Grant stared back, focusing on the eyebrows. It might be fun to paint them, do a whole Frida Kahlo thing. Itty bitty man, big-ass eyebrows slashing across the top of his face.

"Oh, right," the kid said. "The guys."

Grant nodded. "Yep."

The kid opened the rear door of the van. Within the dim interior were two men, each of them almost twice the size of the kid, which made them about Grant's size.

The kid pulled a piece of yellow legal paper from his back pocket, unfolded it, and read, "Carter Varrone, your alpha has sent you here due to your excessive fighting and your inability to peacefully live within your clan or any others. Alex Mathers, your alpha has sent you here for wild and wicked behavior, which includes attacking and—shit, is this for real?"

One of the men in the van growled, low and ominous.

The kid finished in a quiet voice. "—attacking and killing seventeen human women and three shifter women."

The other man inside, Carter Varrone, Grant guessed, gave a whistle and said, "Well, that's fucked up. You're gonna put me in there with that guy?"

"Yeah, you first, Carter," Grant said. Better to do the

easier one first, get the kid more comfortable with the motions of the transfer.

"Fine by me," Carter said, scooting toward the open rear door. He had dark hair, blue eyes, and a devil-may-care attitude. "Lots of assholes to fight in there, right?"

Grant couldn't be sure without naming them all and counting, but he thought there were eleven or twelve guys in the Junkyard. "You're a brawler?" he asked Carter.

Carter bared his teeth. "Fuck yeah. Soothes my bear."

Grant nodded. "It's the perfect spot for you, then. They fight for dominance every damn night, just about."

Carter jumped out of the van, grinning. He was just as muscular as Grant, probably from all the brawling. He turned around to show Grant the zip ties holding his hands behind his back. "You gonna take these off?"

The kid started forward, but Grant held him back.

"He wouldn't hurt us, would he?" the kid asked.

"No promises," Carter said, tilting his head.

Grant sighed. "We're not idiots, Carter. We're not gonna let you go. You'll figure out the zip ties when you're in the yard."

"Whatever." Carter hesitated on the edge of the boundary, the toes of his boots touching the gravel. "Once I go in, I'm in forever, right?"

"Yeah. You need a push?" Grant asked.

"Nah." Shrugging, Carter took two steps over the boundary. He was in.

Well, that wasn't so hard, Grant thought.

The kid looked ready to piss himself with relief.

Carter turned around to face Grant, the kid, and Mathers in the van. Lifting a foot to take the step back again, he said, "I don't feel anything. I think this boundary is bullshit—"

Then he slammed into an invisible barrier.

He shook his head, whipping his dark brown bangs from his eyes. "Fuck, that hurt."

The kid cracked a smile, but Grant looked at Carter.

"You okay, man?" Grant asked.

"Yeah. See you. Or not." Carter loped toward a jagged piece of sheet metal, probably so he could use it to get the zip ties off his wrists.

One down, one to go. Grant was pretty sure Mathers would be a more difficult transfer. He hadn't even come to the edge of the van to face his fate.

"You afraid, Mathers?" Grant asked.

"Hardly. Fuckers chained me to the van."

Either Mathers's alpha was paranoid, or Mathers was a real bad guy. Grant guessed it was the latter, given the things the kid had read off of that paper.

When the kid didn't move to unchain Mathers, Grant sighed. "Hand me the key."

"Thanks, man," the kid said, pulling a key from his pocket and handing it to Grant. "I didn't want to do it."

"You still need to help me get him into the yard," Grant said. "I'm going to unchain him, then together, we push him over the barrier. He probably won't go gently."

"Fuck right, I won't," Mathers growled.

The kid widened his eyes at Grant. He looked like he was about to shit his shorts.

Grant shook his head. "It'll be fine. I've sent big-ass, angry dudes over the boundary before."

He hopped into the van and took a closer look at

Mathers. Brown hair, brown eyes, a cleft chin. Muscles like Grant's. He'd be a fair match if they had to fight. Grant didn't want to fight, he just wanted to go back home to his beer and his painting.

"I'm gonna unchain you now," Grant said, "and I'd appreciate it if you didn't send a foot to my face."

Mathers closed his eyes and echoed Carter's words. "No promises."

Chills raced up Grant's arms, and he didn't scare easily. This was one bad motherfucker. All the better to get him into the Junkyard and let the other bad guys deal with him.

He unlocked Mathers's chains. Luckily, Grant had experience and he was ready to not only block the kick Mathers sent at his head, but come around behind Mathers and grab his neck in a hold that gave him control over the other shifter. He yanked Mathers out of the van with him, grateful that Mathers's wrists were still in the zip ties.

"Fucking motherfucker," Mathers said. "I'll eat your fucking liver."

"You won't be able to get at my fucking liver," Grant said, shoving him toward the boundary but keeping his arm around Mathers's neck. "Kid, get over here, grab his shoulder."

The kid hesitantly took a step forward. "I'm not a kid."

Exasperated, Grant said, "Yeah, okay, will you grab his shoulder?"

Mathers kept up a string of curses and threats, all of which Grant ignored but the kid seemed to take to heart. The kid's grip on Mathers's shoulder looked tenuous at best. Grant grumbled to himself and kept marching Mathers forward. A few more steps.

"Okay, kid, we're gonna hang onto him until I say. He needs to be over the edge completely. Keep your feet braced. Got it?"

"I'm not a kid," the kid said, mouth twisted in a frown.

"Right."

The gravel boundary was one yard away. A foot. Six inches. Mathers fought and twisted the entire way. The gravel border sprayed with the force of his kicking. That wouldn't harm the spell, though. Nothing would, save the intervention of a powerful witch.

Ignoring the dust Mathers kicked up, Grant kept pushing. The kid pushed, too, although with substantially less force. Mathers went lopsided over the gravel border.

As soon as Mathers's feet were over the boundary, the kid let go.

"Wait—" Grant started to shout.

With a roar, Mathers spun around and grabbed Grant's arm.

Fuck.

He didn't feel anything as he went over the line, but he heard the kid shout, "Oh *no*."

Grant looked down. Both of his feet were in the wet earth on the wrong side of the fucking boundary. He leaned back, just to be sure, and his shoulders hit something solid and invisible.

"Mister, I'm so fucking sorry," the kid said.

Grant would've reassured him in some way, but Grant's world had just been changed forever. He thought of his hammock, the porch ceiling that needed painting, the canvases and easels in his garage.

As Mathers grinned and sent a fist flying toward Grant's face, he thought of the fucking beer he had waiting next to the hammock. Grant dodged Mathers's blow, but from the corner of his eye, he saw several shadows emerging from among the scrap metal and junk cars.

Noah Ephraimson, Jase Englander, Damien Buenevista, and several others. All guys Grant had sent over the boundary and into the Junkyard. Even Carter Varrone emerged from behind an old camp trailer.

None of them looked friendly.

Grant was so fucked.

1

Shouts of victory and groans of dismay echoed from the ring. Grant shook his head. They were fighting again—one of the few pastimes available to the guys in the Junkyard. Yeah, someone had fixed up an old car stereo and they could get a handful of radio stations. And books came in along with the food every couple of weeks, although as far as Grant could tell, Stetson Krom was the only guy who read them.

Grant frowned at the view from his trailer. The view was of his beautiful cabin, the place he'd lived until four months ago when Alex Mathers had dragged Grant into the Junkyard after his sorry ass.

Yep. Grant was now living in the very place he'd hated looking at from his front porch. And from this place, he could see the hammock swing lazily in the breeze. The beer he'd left on the porch was long gone, guzzled up by a wandering black bear.

Once he'd gotten free of the other shifters, he'd had to find his own place. Lucky for him, he knew of the trailer, so he'd run toward it and roared at anyone who had chased him. Anyone who underestimated a mountain lion shifter learned fast: the claws were sharp, the jaws powerful.

The trailer was cramped, but clean. It also wasn't as ugly as it used to be—he'd found old cans of paint and even some not-too-crusty brushes in the dump, and he'd painted abstract animals on all four sides of the trailer. His favorite was the mountain lion, of course, but the bear wasn't half bad.

Another set of cheers rose up into the morning sky. "Carter! Carter!"

So the dumbass grizzly was fighting again. Shocker. Nobody seemed to have adjusted so well to life in the Junkyard as Carter Varrone. Dude was in his element. Fights every day, mischief to be wrought at every turn.

Grant was a little jealous, and a little lonely, to be honest.

Four months in the Junkyard, and Grant still hadn't made friends. No big surprise, as he'd shoved most of the guys in here. Carter wasn't bad, and they chatted occasionally, but Carter was just as likely to swing at him as say hello. The guy's inner grizzly was pissed about something. If Grant had any beer, he'd invite Carter over to talk about it, but beer was scarce here. You wanted to get drunk, you drank moonshine made in the back of the 1956 Ford pickup that Noah had claimed.

Grant didn't entirely trust the moonshine wouldn't make him bleed from his eyes, so he kept his distance.

Still, he was bored. He itched to paint, but the old brushes and half-filled cans of house paint weren't calling to him at the moment. He carefully got up from the lawn chair; if he moved too fast, the broken metal on the back would come loose again and the whole thing would fall apart. It helped to lean it against something, so he'd perched it against the front of the trailer. It faced the cabin, which was both a comfort and a torture.

The walk to the ring, in the dump part of the Junkyard, took about five minutes. A chorus of shouting and groans continued during his walk.

"Ooh, ref's here," Jase Englander said. An easygoing guy with dark skin, Jase still liked to stir up trouble. Grant couldn't remember why Jase was in the Junkyard to begin with, but it was Grant's policy not to ask.

Mathers stood up, his brown eyes dark with malice. "You wanna fight again, Lewiston?" he asked, pointing a thick index finger at Grant.

"Nope, just here to watch—what the fuck?"

He'd just taken his first look at the ring, where Carter was matched up against four guys—Damien Buenevista, Derrick Alleman, and a couple other guys Grant didn't know well.

"Keeping things interesting," Mathers said with a laugh.

Four on one might be "interesting" in normal circumstances. But the four were in their animal forms and Carter faced them as a man.

Or rather, he lay on the ground as a man while Buenevista, in his wolf form, grabbed Carter's arm in his jaws and shook his head back and forth like he'd take off the limb.

Shifters could heal from all kinds of shit, but they couldn't grow their arms or legs back.

"This is over," Grant said, starting for the ring.

"The fuck it is." Mathers took a step toward him.

"He's the ref, he makes the rules," Jase said.

"Get out of there," Grant said to the four attacking Carter. He marched forward like he was actually in charge. He wasn't in charge, not really, but he won enough of the nightly battles for dominance that he had some weight to throw around. He could get things for the guys, that was his main pull in the Junkyard. Most of them cared about acquiring the occasional beer or joint. Jase was saving up for a guitar, so he made art and furniture out of recycled materials and depended on a connection to the outside world to sell them. And because Grant didn't actually belong in the Junkyard, he was able to call in favors with the nearby alphas.

"Yeah fine, whatever," Mathers said.

Grant bent down to peer at Carter's face.

"Why'd you fucking interfere?" Carter growled.

"Because you're a fucking idiot with a death wish, that's why."

Carter started to say something else, but coughed instead, spraying blood over Grant's t-shirt.

"Nice," Grant said. "Let's get you up."

He carefully lifted Carter to a standing position so he could walk him back to the weird little cabin Carter had made for himself. It was pretty much smack in the middle of the Junkyard, but that meant it was easy to reach from any part of the territory.

Then he heard it—the fast footfalls of a running human.

A running human *woman*.

Mathers stood up straight and smirked. "I smell pussy."

The same woman had been running past the Junkyard every day for the last two months. When she came by, everyone was careful to either look like they belonged, or to hide. Grant still hadn't laid eyes on her, but her vanilla and rose scent lingered in the air. Some days, it seemed like that scent was the only thing keeping him from losing his mind entirely and succumbing to Mathers's darkness.

Glancing over at Alleman, who had shifted back into his human form and was yanking on a pair of jeans, Mathers said, "You know what to do."

"Wait, what?" Grant said as Alleman took off toward the creek that ran through the territory.

The creek was the closest point to the jogging trail.

"None of your business, asshole," Mathers growled.

Jase shrugged when Grant sent him a questioning look. No answers there.

"It's not good," Carter said, head lolling to the side. "Go."

Grant didn't need to be told twice. He dropped Carter and ran after Alleman. Vaguely, he heard Mathers's running footsteps behind him, but he didn't pay any heed because he had to stop whatever was about to happen.

He arrived at the edge of the creek in time to see Alleman sit down and jab a long piece of metal into his thigh. The wound didn't bleed much, so Alleman yanked the metal out and jabbed again. Blood poured out of the wound, soaking Alleman's jeans.

"The fuck?" Grant said.

The woman was coming up the path. He caught a glimpse of a blond ponytail swishing back and forth. She wore tight, shiny leggings and a loose black tank top layered over a fluorescent green sports bra. Her captivating scent reached his nose. He couldn't believe he was finally looking at the beautiful creature whose scent of roses and vanilla had kept him sane the past few weeks.

"Help!" Alleman called. "Help me!"

The running footsteps faltered as the woman slowed.

"Don't—" Grant started to say, before Mathers's sour odor filled his nostrils and an arm choked off his air.

Grant fell to the ground. The last thing he saw before he blacked out was the bottom of Mathers's boot, coming straight for his face.

2

Caitlyn rounded the bend in the trail she took every day on her afternoon run. Her breathing was even, her legs pleasantly tired. After two months of the same route, she was surprised she even worked up a sweat by the end. She should really challenge herself more, but she wouldn't be in northern California much longer. Now that her aunt had passed, there was nothing holding her here.

This curve would take her past the big scrap yard. Sometimes she saw dudes working in it. Hot dudes. They never called out to her, nor she to them. She felt a strange pull to the scrap yard, but also a push, something holding her back.

A sense of danger, she realized.

"Help! Help me!" a voice called.

Caitlyn slowed. Someone was in danger, and of course she hadn't brought her phone today, thinking that it would be nice, for once, to not worry about getting a call about an emergency back at her aunt's house.

She felt immediately terrible for thinking that way. Her aunt was dead. She should feel more remorse, or at least a sense of loss. She'd lost a lot. Not only her aunt, but her nursing job at the hospital. She didn't miss the job, exactly. It was more that she missed the busyness of it. Because when being busy, she could forget that she had no purpose. No goal. Her estranged aunt's illness had called Caitlyn away from that busy job, and then she'd been left with one job only: caring for her aunt until she died.

There was a lot of quiet when caring for a single sick person. A lot of time to think and ponder life.

Caitlyn hadn't liked all the pondering. Because what her brain had come up with was distressing. Her aunt had never found meaning or real, true love in her life. Caitlyn didn't want to end up that way. Solitude, she could handle. But a life without purpose? Without family? That had been her current trajectory given her schedule at the hospital. No time for friends, family, or fun. She hadn't even come up with a good pun in weeks, and she lived for puns.

As she came toward the bridge that would take her over Cherry Creek, she heard something else, a cut-off, "Don't."

But by now, she could see the man next to the creek. A long, metal pole stuck out of his thigh, and blood spilled from the wound, coating the man's jeans.

"Oh my gosh!" She had to get to him. She leaped over a wide path of gravel, a secondary trail tracing along the edge of the scrap yard. Then she was on her knees next to the man. He smelled foul, like stale beer and sweat.

Filthy Vandal

But a foul odor couldn't keep her from her job. This was a man in need of help—this was an emergency, and Caitlyn was more than able to provide that help. It was her calling. As a nurse, this was what she *did*.

No time to ask him how it happened. She yanked off her tank top and pressed it around the wound, hoping to stanch the bleeding.

"How deep does it go?" she asked.

The man turned a surprisingly clear pair of eyes to her face, then flicked them down to her breasts, which were encased in her modest sports bra. Licking his lips, he leered at her.

The hell? She'd dealt with a lot of creeps, but generally if a guy had an injury as bad as a giant metal rod stuck in his leg and was bleeding all over the place, he didn't take the time to check her out.

Someone grabbed her arms and yanked them behind her. A rough voice said, "Hello, pretty one."

Caitlyn screamed. The guy in front of her pulled the pole out of his leg and tossed it aside. Then he stood up.

He stood the fuck up.

She couldn't believe her eyes. He was bleeding. The blood had been real. She'd heard the sick squelch as he removed the metal from his thigh.

"Ruined a damn fine pair of jeans for this, Mathers," the man said.

"Oh, just shift already so you can heal faster," the man holding her said.

Caitlyn had forgotten to struggle at the sight of the guy pulling the pole from his leg and standing up, but she tried stomping on the instep of her assailant now. He easily dodged her.

"I get a fair chance of mating her, yeah?" the injured guy said as he yanked off his jeans.

"What the hell is going on?" Caitlyn asked. "Let go of me. Immediately."

They both laughed. A couple of other guys came up, openly staring at her. She'd pulled off her tank without a second thought, hoping to staunch the bleeding of the fallen man, and now she felt exposed. Naked. Powerless.

This was bullshit.

"Everyone gets a chance," the guy behind her, Mathers, said. "We'll fight for her. Ultimate prize."

"I don't fucking think so—" Caitlyn started to say.

One of the other guys, a giant with an unkempt beard, jammed a dirty piece of cloth into her mouth.

Rough rope came around her wrists, and then more around her legs. She kicked hard. She was strong. She didn't have to put up with this. She'd hop back onto the trail and go for help, report what these assholes were doing.

But that was imaginary. Because the reality was that she was totally in their power and she had no way of escaping. And she was not only scared, but pissed. Angry tears filled her eyes. How could she have gotten into this situation? The man had been impaled by a giant fucking piece of metal. She hadn't imagined that.

He was naked now, she saw as someone swung her around. Not only naked, but crouching on the ground. A strange light was surrounding him. Had she hit her head at some point? Maybe the cloth in her mouth was coated in some kind of hallucinogen.

When the light faded, a mountain lion stood in his place. A gash on its hind leg was closing up before her eyes.

This wasn't real. She struggled to bring in air, something to help her see better, to allow her mind to work, because obviously she wasn't getting enough oxygen through the rag in her mouth. It tasted like dirt and sweat.

She couldn't breathe.

Someone lifted her into the air. The world went dark.

Consciousness returned to her when someone set her down on cool linoleum. She blinked her eyes open, her heart already picking up its pace again. It looked like she was in a narrow building, maybe a camp trailer. Grimy windows let in a tiny bit of light and illuminated the filthy floor she sat on, and a lump of cushions or trash bags rested in the corner.

The cloth was still jammed in her mouth. She focused on breathing through her nose, slowly and evenly. Panic wasn't going to help her in this situation. Thinking clearly just might help.

Some kind of hallucinogen was in the rag, apparently. She had to get rid of it.

A man stood in front of her in dirty jeans and a camo tank. He bent down so his face was closer to hers. He smelled like the guy who'd been holding her from behind. Mathers, was his name. He had a cleft chin that was mostly covered in whiskers. His brown hair was greasy and in desperate need of a trim, and his dark brown eyes gave her the chills.

He grinned, but not a reassuring kind of grin. It was more the kind of grin you'd see on Hannibal Lecter before he cut into a very rare steak.

He said, "You can run, pretty, but there's less than a hundred acres in this junkyard, and we'll catch you again quick. I suggest you don't piss us off, but honestly, lots of guys here like a little chase."

If her mouth wasn't so dry because of the rag, she would have gulped in fear. She forced herself to keep still.

Humming to himself, Mathers stood up straight and walked out of the trailer.

Tears leaked from Caitlyn's eyes. Nobody would miss her, nobody would come looking for her. Aunt Galinda had passed. The estate was all in Caitlyn's name and she hadn't decided what to do with it. Electricity was paid for the next month. Her friends down south knew that she was busy up here, and she wasn't that close to them to begin with. She hadn't talked to a soul other than the attorney after her aunt's passing.

A noise reached her ears from across the little trailer. She looked up in alarm. The pile of trash bags was *breathing*. Was that a man? She squinted, trying to see better, but all she could make out was a big, lumpy mass. It was definitely big enough to be human.

"Hey," she whispered. "Hey, wake up."

The mass continued breathing.

What if that man—or woman—was worse than Mathers? Maybe it would be best to let the person sleep.

She moved her wrists back and forth behind her, hoping to stretch the rope. If nobody was coming to look for her, she'd best rescue herself. Someway, somehow, she'd get out of here.

3

It was dark when Grant woke up. He was on his side, on the floor. He could see a wall right in front of him.

His arms hurt. When he tried to move them, they pulled against rope. He'd been tied up. He could try shifting, but first he wanted to know where he was and what was going on.

The sounds outside were of more fighting in the ring. A few people shouted and booed, and Mathers announced, "Jase lost. Noah's the next contender for taking the bitch."

The bitch? Had they convinced the runner to come over the boundary line? Shit. They must have. And now they were fighting over her—she was the prize. A dull ache spread through Grant at the thought.

He guessed he was in Mathers's trailer. It smelled sour, like rotting citrus, so Grant was pretty sure about his guess. Still, he rolled over, as carefully as possible, so he could see the room behind him.

Filthy Vandal

Whoa. There she was. The woman who'd traipsed over the boundary to "help" Alleman. She was sleeping, her head lolling to one side, her eyes closed. Her arms were behind her back, probably tied there, and a rag was stuffed in her mouth. Why they would bother gagging her, Grant had no idea—it wasn't like anyone would hear her if she started screaming. The trail she ran on every day—she'd been the only person to use it since before Grant had come to work at the Junkyard.

Dried tear tracks ran down her face.

Grant's heart gave a painful squeeze in his chest. This wasn't right.

"Hey, lady," he said. "Hey."

Her eyes shot open. She looked wildly around the trailer until her gaze landed on him. Immediately, she began scooting away, putting more distance between them.

"I'm not going to hurt you," Grant said. "My name is Grant. I'd like to help."

He wanted to know her name, but she wouldn't be able to tell him until he helped her with the gag.

He'd have to shift in front of her to get free of his rope. She was human, though, and he doubted she'd react well to seeing a full-grown mountain lion standing in front of her. Still, there was no other choice.

"When are you gonna fight, huh, Mathers?" one of the guys said. "Pussying out on us?"

"Bidin' my time," Mathers said.

"Waiting for us all to get tired so *you* can claim her, more like," the guy said.

Thwack. The sound of a solid hit. Then the thud of a person falling.

Mathers said, "Anyone else want to fuckin' argue with me?"

Silence.

"Then let's go. Ephraimson and Alleman. Begin."

Cheers rose up once more.

Grant looked at the woman again. Her brown eyes were dark with misery and hopelessness. He guessed he'd been unconscious most of the afternoon, and she'd likely been struggling, wondering what was going to happen to her.

"I'm gonna try to get us out of here," Grant told her. He wasn't sure how to prepare her for the sight of him shifting. "This might be scary—"

The trailer door opened and a shadow filled the frame. Grant looked up, saw Carter. Great, just what he needed—someone to cause more mischief.

A knife caught the faint light shining through one of the windows, and Carter strode on silent feet toward Grant. The woman made sounds of panic and dismay, but Carter simply cut the ropes that held Grant's arms in place.

"Thanks, man," Grant said.

"Not doing it for you," Carter said.

"You know I'm just going to free the woman," Grant said, eyeing Carter suspiciously.

Carter shrugged. "Go for it, I don't care. I like my women willing, not tied up and won in a fight."

Grant agreed.

"Why are you doing this, anyway?" Grant asked as he rolled up to his feet.

"The others are gonna lose their shit when you take off with her," Carter said. "I find it fucking amusing. Whoever leaves with her tonight, keeps her. Mathers said. So if you leave, you keep her, and they don't get her. Everyone's gonna be pissed. Blood will fly."

"Is that why you didn't join the fights? You wanted to save her instead?"

"Could be. But I love a good tussle. I'm going out there now." With a smirk, Carter ducked back out of the trailer and disappeared into the shadows of metal scraps.

The woman stared up at Grant with her brown eyes wide and questioning.

"Let's get you out of here. Try to keep quiet, though," Grant said, and yanked the rag from her mouth.

She swallowed several times and took some deep breaths. He wanted to hear her voice, but he didn't want the others to hear a feminine voice and know she was free.

He helped her stand. Her legs shook, so he did his best to support her while not touching her too much. He didn't want to spook her.

Carter had left the knife on the counter, so Grant used it to cut the woman's ropes and then kept hold of it. If he needed to fight for her, he would, and he had zero interest in fighting clean at this point. Informal referee or not, he'd do whatever it took to keep her safe.

He didn't know why he felt so responsible for her, but he could cogitate on that later.

"Come on," he whispered, and went to the door of the

trailer. He paused there, listening for anyone who might be waiting, but all was silent on the other side of the door. Everyone was busy with the fighting.

He kept to the shadows and prayed the woman had enough sense to do the same. They skirted around large sheets of corrugated metal, old cars piled against each other, and giant, rust-coated cans.

While he skulked around an old pick-up, he kept his attention on the woman. She was obviously uncomfortable and looked ready to bolt at any moment. Still, she kept her focus and followed him away from the scrap yard and into the cover of the trees along the boundary of the Junkyard. When she opened her mouth to say something, probably believing they were out of earshot of the others, he shook his head and held a finger to his lips. Nodding, she didn't speak.

They were nearly to his trailer when she stopped suddenly. Grant stopped, too, and looked at her in question.

Can we talk now? she mouthed.

"Yeah," he said quietly, "but we should really keep moving—"

"A question, first." Hands on her hips, she asked, "What did they put in that gag?"

He stared at her, perplexed. "It was just a dirty rag."

"No, there was something in it."

"Grease, maybe?" If she was going to be finicky about dirt, she was going to have a hard time adjusting to the Junkyard. He went on. "Maybe oil? The rag was probably used to clean up after playing with cars; Luca leaves those rags everywhere."

She shook her head, and her ponytail swung angrily behind her. "No. There was something else in that rag. Something that made me hallucinate."

Oh, shit. He thought he knew where this was going. "We...we don't have any drugs here. Other than weed, I mean. Some alcohol, and that shit is strong, but it won't make you hallucinate. I can guess what you saw, babe, and it wasn't a hallucination."

"I'm not your *babe*, and it *was* a hallucination."

He held up his hands. "Okay."

No sense in trying to convince her about shifters now. She'd find out soon enough.

4

When the man, Grant, continued through the trees, Caitlyn followed him. It wasn't like she had much of a choice, did she? She could bolt—she was a fast runner—but then she'd be lost in the forest in the dark. She would just as likely run to freedom as run straight back into Mathers's trailer. Or fall into Cougar Lake.

They approached a different trailer. Her night vision wasn't great, but the moon was bright enough to see by. It was a tiny camp trailer and looked barely big enough for one person. Someone had painted the outside of it with swirling animal shapes. They weren't idealized visions of wildlife, either, but swirling and beautiful and awful all at once. A part of her wanted to stop and stare at the artwork, but her survival instinct kicked in, thankfully. She needed to get far away from this place, as quickly as possible.

"Look," she said, "if you can just let me borrow your phone, I'll find someone to give me a ride out of here."

The guy frowned. "I know you have no reason to trust me. None at all. In your place, I wouldn't trust me, either. But I have no phone, and nobody can get you out of here tonight."

"Are you for real?"

He didn't sound like he was lying, but seriously, who didn't have a phone?

"I'm for real," he said. "Can you try something, just really quickly, for me?"

"It depends on what," she said.

"Can you try to put your hand over here?" He pointed to a tree.

She reached for it, but her hand met resistance. The resistance was smooth, not the bark of a tree, more like a smooth wall. "I'm still hallucinating," she murmured, pulling her hand back quickly.

"I wish," he said, just as quietly.

She swayed on her feet. She hadn't eaten since lunch, hadn't had a drop of water to drink, and she was tired through to her bones.

"Okay," he said. "You look exhausted. You can sleep inside. I'll stay outside and guard the door. They're not going to be happy I walked off with you, and it's better this way."

Looking at the rundown trailer, she was half-tempted to volunteer to sleep outside, too. She expected the place would smell sour and rank like the other trailer. But there was a bite to the June evening. It wouldn't hurt to look inside and see if there were blankets, at the very least.

"So, we'll be safe?" she asked.

"Lady, I haven't been safe since I got here four months

ago." He gave a bark of sarcastic laughter, then sobered up and said, "But you'll be safe enough. I'll make sure of it."

Nodding, she went up to the trailer door. She was too tired to ask questions, too tired to understand what was happening. She wasn't too tired to notice that Grant was super hot. Even in the dim light, she could see his strong jaw line and soulful eyes. His eyebrows were crooked like he was angry, but the self-effacing grin on his face softened the expression.

She had to tamp down her feelings, because this wasn't the time and it sure as hell wasn't the place to be ogling some random dude who had supposedly "won" her by walking off with her to another trailer in the woods.

Tomorrow. She would ask questions tomorrow.

A round of wood served as a step to the door of the trailer. The door itself was unlocked, so she pulled it open and stuck her head inside. Instead of reeking of rancid lemons like that other trailer, it smelled very faintly of cleaner. The floor reflected moonlight. There wasn't much space, but a tiny counter lined the wall, pointing the way to a bed that was neatly made with a plaid quilt. She turned around and looked at Grant in surprise. "It's nice in here."

He shrugged. "I like to keep a clean place. There's a bathroom at the side, there. And the taps work, if you're thirsty. Food in the cupboards is all yours if you want it."

"Thanks." His kindness made her feel weak in the knees. Wow, she'd had a day if this was how she reacted to someone offering her food and a place to sleep. She blinked back tears and her throat ached with emotion. She *had* had a day. She'd been freaking kidnapped and—and—

"Hey, now," he said, stepping up next to her. "It's going to be all right."

She was crying. Dammit.

"Do you want a hug?" he asked. "It's killing me not to hug you when you're sad, but I don't want to freak you out..."

She launched herself at him and felt his warm, kind arms surround her. It was like being embraced by a sunlit boulder. Hot. Hard. Safe. The comforting sound of his heartbeat thumped beneath her ear. It sounded a little faster than a resting heart rate. Her heart was beating faster, too. But they'd just hurried through the woods. That's all. It wasn't that their hearts were in any way excited to be so close.

Her tears stopped while she thought about those things, and she realized the hug had gone on far too long.

"Thanks," she said, pulling back.

He dropped his arms. "You're welcome. I needed it, too. Glad we could get you away from Mathers. Get some rest, okay? There are clean clothes in there, wear whatever you want."

She gave him a brief smile before stepping the rest of the way into the trailer and closing the door behind her. Hot or not, he wasn't sleeping with her tonight. He'd offered to stay outside, and she'd let him.

But after finding a long-sleeved shirt of his to put on, then drinking a glass of water and climbing into a bed that smelled of clean fabric and hazelnut, she wondered how it would feel to fall asleep with those muscled arms around her.

The snarls and growls of fighting animals filled her dreams, but when she fully awoke in the light of morning, all was quiet outside save for the birds' morning chorus.

She stretched and her arm hit the edge of the trailer. The noise shocked her out of her sleepy stupor. Where the hell was she?

"What the hell just happened?" she wondered aloud. She'd been kidnapped and she'd trusted some random dude to let her sleep in his camp trailer instead of demanding he return her to civilization so she could file a police report and several restraining orders.

The morning air bit into her skin, but her anger kept her warm enough so she ignored the jacket dangling from a wall hook and stormed outside. Grant's long-sleeved shirt would have to be enough.

Grant sat on a picnic chair that looked like it could barely hold his weight. He leaned against the side of the trailer and turned to look at her when she came out. "Morning," he croaked.

"I need answers, and I need them right the fuck now," she said.

"Fine," he said, looking more awake.

She took in the sight of him. His shirt was torn at the sleeve, and a scratch ran across his shoulder, deep and angry-looking.

"We'll start with what happened to you," she said in a softer voice. Her anger was fading at the sight of his injury.

"It's fine," he said. "It'll heal soon."

She doubted it, but if he didn't want to talk about it, she had other questions. "Look, I need the truth. No half-truths, no evasion. Just tell me what's going on. Please."

He stared back at her with eyes that were the color of pine trees. She hadn't been able to see their color at night, and now she was struck with just how beautiful they were.

"I'm going to tell you the truth," he said slowly, "but you aren't gonna believe it."

"Stranger than fiction?" she asked.

He gave a short laugh. "Something like that. Do you believe in the supernatural?"

"Nope. Science girl through and through." Although she'd seen some odd things in the course of her short nursing career. Patients who swore they saw ghosts in the hospital's hallways or rooms. Others who talked about mystical beings. Vampires. Werewolves. She'd met more than one practicing Wiccan. But there were other patients who were convinced they were Elvis, or spouted conspiracy theories about everything from flower pollen to soup cans.

"Well, everything happening right now is rooted in the supernatural," Grant said.

"Right," she said slowly. "Go ahead, spit it out."

"Fine. You're in a magical holding pen for misbehaving shapeshifters, and none of us can get out."

What? Who the hell did this guy think he was? Who

did he think *she* was? She knew who she was, and her personality traits didn't include "gullible."

"Fuck you," she said, voice shaking.

It was light now, and she could find her own way back to the trail. She didn't need this beautiful dickhead's help.

Aiming west, opposite the rising sun, she began to run.

5

Fuck.

"Wait," Grant called.

He didn't even know her name.

Fighting with the guys last night had been brutal. His side ached from a solid hit Mathers had dealt him. Grant had come out on top, but just barely.

Aches and pains or not, he took off after the woman.

She was fast, but he had his shifter speed on his side, so he caught up with her about three yards from the gravel that delineated the boundary of the Junkyard. She spun to face him.

"Look, I get that you're pissed, you don't believe me," he said. Then he pointed at the wall. "But you do *not* want to run smack into the barrier."

She looked at him like he was crazy. Fair enough.

"Here, watch." He strode to the gravel line, pulled back his hand, and slapped the wall. His palm took the impact. It smarted. He rubbed his hand all over the invisible wall, following it. High above his head, it curved slightly inward, like it was domed. "See?"

"I see an amateur mime," she said. "Cool trick."

He could only imagine how he looked to her. He bit back a laugh.

She started forward, shaking her head.

"Wait," he said. "Just...stick out your hand before you walk into it."

Muttering several swear words under her breath, she put out her arm and walked forward.

Her hand hit the invisible wall. "What—"

She pushed out with her hand again, and again met resistance. She turned to Grant, her expression perplexed and pissed.

He wasn't a portrait painter, but he'd love to capture the flash in her chocolate-brown eyes. Human or not, this woman was a force to be reckoned with.

"We can't get out," he said.

"What—is—this—bullshit?" she said, pounding against the barrier with her fist.

"You're gonna bruise your hand."

"I need to get out of here!"

"Lady, we *all* want to get out of here. But we can't. I'm going to talk to a guy, see if he can find a witch. Maybe she'll know how to let you out without letting the others go." He'd hope the witch would make an allowance for an unwitting human. And while that allowance was being made, perhaps the witch would let Grant leave, too. Couldn't hurt to ask.

The woman walked along the gravel line, hand out and following the invisible wall. She stopped every few steps and stood on tiptoes to touch the wall high up, then squatted to run her hands along the bottom of it.

"We've all done that," Grant said. "Every single shifter here has walked the boundary of the Junkyard."

Except maybe Carter. That asshole seemed to like it in here.

She ignored him and kept feeling along the wall.

"If you keep going," he said, "it'll take you straight to the scrap yard and Mathers's trailer."

That got her to stop. Her eyebrows pulled together as she scowled. "How high up does it go?"

"It curves in. We think it's like a dome, but we don't know how high the top is. I can climb trees in the center of the territory without ever reaching a barrier, so we think it goes pretty high. Not that it matters. The point is, we can't climb over it."

"You're saying I'm stuck here."

"We all are. It's impossible to get out."

She nodded, obviously thinking it over. "How long?"

"I don't know..."

"No, how long have you been here?"

"Me? Four months. Mathers and Carter, the same. Stetson's the newest, he came in March. Ephraimson—Noah—he's been here longest. Couple of years." Grant had shoved every single one of these guys, except for Stetson, in here himself. Nobody had taken over Grant's post after Mathers had tugged him over the boundary. Alphas had to make their own men do the dirty work.

When the woman didn't say anything, Grant said, "What's your name?"

"Caitlyn Dorsey."

"Caitlyn." He liked how it sounded. "I'm going to try to keep you as comfortable as possible, okay?"

"That's what hospitals say to terminal patients."

"It's not like that," he said. "I'll keep you safe, away from the other guys. And I'm going to try to find a way for you to get out of here."

"You just told me it's impossible." She walked past him, back toward his trailer, shoulders down, head down, defeated.

She sat outside the trailer in the spot where he'd spent the night. Her gaze never left the cabin straight ahead that sat on the other side of the wall.

"Do you want to talk?" he asked.

"No."

Taking her at her word, he went inside and fixed a breakfast of English muffins and peanut butter. He sliced an apple and divided it up, arranging the crescents along the edges of the plates. The fresh food was running low—they were due for a new shipment of food and other necessities. It was Hutchins's turn to send it, so Grant knew it would be a good shipment. Some alphas were assholes and sent the bare minimum to the Junkyard. Nonperishables, primarily. Nothing good. Guys like Hutchins, though, or Gabe Fournier, would put in fresh fruit and vegetables. Even better, Hutchins's son, Phillip, would probably do the delivery, and Grant would be able to ask him to call a witch.

He came back out of the trailer and handed a plate to Caitlyn. She nodded her thanks.

She'd said she didn't want to talk, so he sat on the ground next to her lawn chair and they both looked at his old cabin. Wildflowers grew in front of it, where he'd spread seed a year ago. The place, despite starting to look rundown, was picturesque. He thought of all his paints in the garage, his canvases and brushes. Phillip had brought him a sketchbook and charcoals last time he was here, but it wasn't the same.

Grant didn't know what Caitlyn was thinking, exactly, but he had a pretty good idea how she felt right now.

And they still hadn't one hundred percent discussed the concept of shapeshifters.

From the dull look in Caitlyn's eyes, this wasn't a good time.

He ate all of the food on his plate, but Caitlyn didn't touch hers.

"Are you going to eat?" he asked her.

She shook her head and tried to hand him her plate.

"Nah, keep it," he said. "You might get hungry in a little while."

They sat together in silence for what felt like forever. Grant wanted to learn about her, more than just her name. But she just stared ahead at the cabin.

After some time, his ass was completely numb. He stood up, wincing. Caitlyn stood up, too. She marched to the gravel line and pushed outward with both hands until they couldn't go any farther forward. Then she sank to her knees and leaned her forehead against the wall.

"Come here," Grant said, reaching for her elbow.

She shook him off. "Just leave me alone."

He couldn't leave her unprotected. Last night's battle had ensured he was the victor and alpha of the territory for at least a little while longer, but he had no doubt that if he left her alone entirely, someone else would come along and take her away. Still, she wanted solitude. He'd take a short walk around his trailer and do what he could for her.

As he walked away, the sound of other footsteps reached his ears and he went on immediate alert. Sniffing the air, he caught the scent of grizzly and rosewood. Carter.

A moment later, Carter stepped out of the shadows. He jerked his chin toward Caitlyn, who was still kneeling at the boundary and looking at the trees and cabin on the other side. "What's up with her?"

"What do you think, asshole? She just found out she can't escape."

"It's not so bad in here," Carter said.

Grant shook his head. Of course Carter wouldn't understand. "Dude, she won't eat."

"'Course she won't. Did you have an appetite when Mathers dragged you in? Did any of us?"

Maybe Carter understood more than Grant had thought. "I guess not."

"But she'll get used to it," Carter went on. "It's pretty here. Let her get to know you, and maybe she'll fall in love with you and you can make a perfect little family."

"In the fuckin' Junkyard?" Grant said, horrified. His chest hurt at the thought of everything he'd lost when Mathers had dragged him in. Grant didn't have a mate and he hadn't had designs on anyone, but he'd known someday he might want a family. He'd put those notions to rest soon after finding out none of the alphas would try to free him.

Grant wasn't worth freeing, but Caitlyn was.

Carter was smirking at him. Smug bastard.

"You always have to stir shit up, don't you?" Grant asked.

"Sorry," Carter said as he walked away.

But the apology was empty, which they both knew.

Turning around, Grant looked at Caitlyn, who still sat next to the boundary. Her blond ponytail drooped down her back like a flag of defeat.

Grant had to talk to a witch as soon as possible. Not for himself, though. He'd lost hope a long time ago for himself. This would be for Caitlyn. He'd stay in here forever, if only Caitlyn could go free.

6

When she woke the next morning, Caitlyn made a decision. Enough moping. So she was (maybe) stuck here for (maybe) forever. And it wasn't fine. It wasn't okay. But was she going to sit against the invisible wall every day and feel sorry for herself, or was she going to live the best life she could under the circumstances?

Easy choice, but hard to do.

She made the bed and checked herself out in the cracked mirror hanging on the outside of the bathroom door. She didn't look nearly as wrecked as she felt. Good. She brushed her teeth with her finger and some toothpaste she found in one of the drawers near the sink. Experimenting, she tugged her lips upward in a smile. It was almost convincing. She kept the fake smile on her face while she fixed her hair back into a high ponytail. She'd heard that smiling, even when you're unhappy, can lift your mood. And she was ready to try every trick in the proverbial book.

After blowing herself a kiss in the mirror, she went outside to face the world.

Grant was sitting outside the trailer again. This morning, a deep gash marred his cheekbone.

"What happened?" she asked. "And how's your shoulder from yesterday?"

"The shoulder is fine," he said, taking in her appearance. Something about his gaze caused little flickers of pleasure in her belly. He didn't leer at her like the other guys had done. "You're looking better."

See, the fake smile had worked. "Thanks. But your shoulder?"

"It's fine. Already healed up."

"No, I should've tended to it yesterday, but let me take a look now." She'd been selfishly involved in her own struggles and completely ignored the injured person right in front of her. If the wound got infected, how would they treat it? It wasn't like they could rush to the hospital.

He lifted up his sleeve. "It's already gone, see?"

His muscular bicep was distracting and entirely unscathed. Maybe she'd mixed up which arm had been hurt. "Show me your other one."

Grinning, he turned and lifted his other sleeve. More tanned skin covering perfect muscles. Not even a scar in sight.

"Tell me what's going on," she said. "This shouldn't be possible."

"I told you about magic." His voice was quiet, his green eyes guarded.

"Magic healed you?" She reached tentatively toward

his arm. When he didn't draw back, she smoothed her palm over his skin.

The contact made her breath catch in her throat and she yanked her hand away. A feeling. More than a feeling—a need. It swirled through her lower abdomen, gathering heat.

"What...?" She looked into his eyes.

He looked nearly as surprised as she felt. "What did you just do?"

"I don't know. Nothing." Her heart pounded away in her chest, double-time. She would probably break the blood pressure machine she'd used to monitor her aunt's declining health if she were to hook herself up to it right now. Holding her hand out once more, she said, a half-smile on her face, "Can I touch you again? For science?"

He snickered, which gave her a jolt of pleasure. She liked amusing him, apparently, although she had no idea why.

"I am a nurse," she murmured. "I worked in a hospital and everything." Reaching out again, she touched his upper arm. Again, that feeling of need and desire flowed through her veins.

Grant nodded, as if a question had been answered, but she didn't remember asking him one.

"Can I touch *you*?" he asked. "Also, you know, for science."

"Sure."

She held out her arm. Instead of running his palm over it like she'd expected, he grabbed her and yanked her into his lap. She let out a shout of surprise.

"You okay?" he asked.

"No, you just *manhandled* me, you big brute." But strangely, she didn't mind. Both of his hands were on her arms, gliding over her skin, igniting that warm feeling of need in her once again.

She risked a glance at his face, which was now so close to hers, she could kiss him if she wanted to.

And she kind of wanted to.

From the heavy-lidded gaze of his green eyes, which tracked from her eyes to her lips, he wanted the same thing.

"What's going on?" she whispered.

"Fate, I think."

Whoa, that was deep, and kind of sudden. She stared hard at his face, looking for a sign that he was joking, but he looked dead serious.

He rubbed his hands up and down her arms again. She held back a sigh of want. His dick was hard, poking into her ass. Knowing it was there, that he was as turned on as she was, made her want to adjust her position so she was straddling him.

If this was Fate, as he'd guessed it was, then she was hoping Fate came equipped with a box of condoms and plenty of lube.

His mouth was right there. Right freaking there. All she had to do was stretch her neck a tiny bit and—*yes*.

The kiss was scorching from the second her lips touched his. He gave her two chaste pecks before turning his head so their mouths slotted together like they'd been formed for no other purpose than to kiss each other. When his lips parted slightly and his tongue came forward to touch hers, she opened her mouth and allowed him in. He tasted like hazelnut and campfire. She couldn't get enough. Using his shoulders, she braced herself and turned around in his lap, never once breaking apart from their kiss.

He gripped the back of her borrowed shirt in his fists, tightening it against her chest—so tight it was like he was holding her breasts in his palms. Although he hadn't touched her there yet, she couldn't wait until he did.

Everything. She would give him everything.

"Soooo...this is new."

The voice startled them out of the kiss. Caitlyn started to struggle off of Grant's lap, but he held her fast. When she kept resisting, he let her go and she stood, turning to face the intruder.

"Carter." Grant's voice was a growl and it sounded like it belonged to an animal, not a man.

The other man, Carter, held up his hands. He had dark hair and blue eyes that pierced the morning light. His mouth quirked with amusement. "Sorry to interrupt you two. Just thought you should know that Mathers and them are less than thrilled you claimed the woman, Grant. They're saying if you don't give her up, they'll take her themselves, and they won't be fighting you one on one."

"Claimed...the woman?" Caitlyn said, struggling to come out of the kissing fog to understand Carter's words.

"Yeah, he didn't tell you?" Carter asked. "By walking off with you the other night, he won the contest and you're his now."

Caitlyn spun on her heel to face Grant. "What?"

Now that her mind was clearing, she remembered

something about that. She'd been the prize, and whoever walked away with her was the winner. She'd somehow forgotten that over the past twenty-four hours, but now that Carter had brought it up, she was angry. Because here she was, about to hand over her vagina like some kind of trophy to the "winner."

Not anymore.

"Thanks, Carter," Grant said in a voice that said he was anything but grateful. "Really appreciate it. Now scram."

Laughing, Carter walked away.

Caitlyn kept her gaze on Grant. "I'm *yours*, huh?"

"As far as they're concerned, yes. As far as you're concerned, no. It was a technicality I used to help keep you safe."

A technicality she'd forgotten about. And then they'd kissed each other breathless.

"We need to talk about this," Caitlyn began.

"Phillip's here early," he said.

"Phillip?"

"The guy who can contact a witch for us. I can hear his truck."

Caitlyn listened, but all she heard was faint birdsong.

"I can hear better than you," he said. "I'll try to explain it on the way...if you'll listen."

When he held out his hand, she took it automatically. She wanted to be close to him, despite the weirdness, despite the whole "prize" thing Carter had brought up. Nothing Carter said could change their kiss or the way her body craved his.

As they walked, Grant said, "You didn't believe me

yesterday, about magic. But I also said something else. I told you the magic wall is here to keep in misbehaving shapeshifters."

Caitlyn kept her eyes ahead. Shapeshifters sounded like something out of a supernatural show about mercurial gods.

And he'd said something about *shifters*, too, but she'd only been half-listening at that point, trying to wrap her mind around this place.

"And that's what the Junkyard is," Grant went on. "It's like a supernatural holding ground, or exile. The shifter thing wasn't a lie, I wasn't joking around. All the guys in here, we can change into animals, and it's why I can hear that truck from far away and you can't. My shapeshifting ability gives me stronger senses."

Caitlyn heard him, she was listening. She just wasn't sure what to think.

They reached a small clearing next to a pond that looked barely deep enough to swim in. Still, the sight of the water sparkling in the sunlight was beautiful.

The sound of cheering rose up in the distance, and she finally heard the truck.

"He's going to toss the goods over to us," Grant said, "and the guys'll divide them up. I'll get mine later. Then Phillip will come around to meet with me. We can just wait here for him, if you want. But Caitlyn. Please, talk to me."

She allowed him to tug her to a fallen tree, its trunk old and worn free of bark. They leaned against it. She sensed his gaze on her, but she focused on the ground, on a purple and white columbine flower swaying in the breeze.

"I think it's a lot to take in," she finally said. "I need a week or two to wrap my head around all of this."

"Hopefully we'll have you out before then."

"And you, too?" she asked. She hadn't been conscious of the concern until it came out of her mouth.

He shrugged, his massive shoulders moving up and down. "I was dragged in here by mistake, so it would be great to get out. But I'm more worried about you. I accepted this months ago, but you shouldn't have to."

She didn't want to leave him behind.

Insanity. She shouldn't feel a pang at the thought of going off without him—she didn't even know this guy.

"Tell me more about you," she said, trying to cover up the strange feelings swirling around in her heart.

"Not sure what to tell. My animal's a mountain lion—that's what I turn into."

"What's that like?" she asked. "Are you still you when you...transform?"

"Yeah, it's still me in here. But sometimes the lion's like an extra consciousness I have. It has urges of its own, but those urges are always good for me, too."

"Urges?"

"Like, the urge to be closer to you. My inner mountain lion is roaring with the need to be with you."

She couldn't help but feel weirdly flattered by that strange-as-hell sentiment.

"What else?" she asked.

"That cabin you kept staring at—that's my place.

Right outside the boundary. It's where I lived before Mathers pulled me into the Junkyard."

"That's yours? It's beautiful." She'd been thinking, while she'd stared at it, that it looked like the perfect little place to live. Out in the quiet, in the woods. No more busy city hospital. She'd miss her nursing career in a place like that, but it would be nice to escape to for long vacations.

"Here he comes," Grant said.

Caitlyn followed Grant's gaze to a space along the gravel line that delineated the boundary wall. A young man approached. He wore faded jeans and a t-shirt, and a baseball cap sat backward on his head.

"Lewiston," the guy said.

"The younger Hutchins," Grant said. "How the hell are ya?"

"I'm good." He nodded to Caitlyn and took off his hat. "Miss, it's nice to meet you. I'm Phillip Hutchins."

"Hi," Caitlyn said. "Caitlyn Dorsey. I'd offer to shake hands, but..."

Phillip grimaced.

"Now do you believe me that it's not just bad guys trapped in here?" Grant said to Phillip. He turned to Caitlyn and added, "This asshole thought maybe I deserved my fate when Mathers pulled me in. He thought the spell only kept in bad guys. But you can't think that now, can you, Phillip? Caitlyn's human, and she's a nurse—not a murderer or pervert."

"I could be a pervert," Caitlyn said, batting her eyelashes at Grant.

Phillip blushed, and they all laughed.

"Nah, I believe you now," Phillip said. "The others said a woman had come in."

"Assholes tricked her. Alleman and Mathers, both of them." Grant's friendly expression darkened.

Phillip nodded. "Yeah, they said. Mathers was proud. We'll have to close the jogging trail so it doesn't happen again."

"So, you'll find us a witch?" Grant asked.

"I'll call one now. No promises she'll do anything." Phillip pulled a phone from his pocket, tapped the screen a few times, and held the phone to his ear. "Hey, Maddie. Yeah. We have a situation at the Junkyard."

Caitlyn and Grant waited while he explained the "situation," which Caitlyn thought would be more aptly described as a "catastrophe." Caitlyn interrupted Phillip to explain that both she and Grant should be let out, not just her.

"So you'll do it?" Phillip asked the witch, then waited. "Conditions?"

"Wait—have her text you the conditions," Grant said. "I don't want the others to overhear."

Caitlyn looked around them. They appeared to be alone, but Grant must have heard that truck from a mile away. He could probably hear others nearby, even if they were hiding.

"Thanks," Phillip said into the phone. "Bye."

A moment later, his phone buzzed and he held the screen up near the barrier so Caitlyn and Grant could see it.

Will meet you at the boundary by the pond in two days. Dawn. Bring a piece of white crystal as payment.

A white crystal? Caitlyn wondered. "What's—"

"Shh," Grant said. "Later. Some of them are here."

He waved to Phillip, whose eyes got big as he looked past Caitlyn. He took a step back.

"Good luck," Phillip said. As if he was afraid to witness what came next, he turned and hurried away from the border.

"Caitlyn," Grant said in a soft, yet urgent, tone, "you're gonna need to run to the trailer, okay? Go inside and lock the door behind you."

She risked a glance behind her and saw a grizzly at the edge of the little clearing. When she gasped, it roared and charged toward them.

7

Caitlyn took one look at the approaching grizzly and Grant didn't need to tell her twice. She ran. Unfortunately for Grant, the grizzly—Mathers—was fully animal and Grant was still in his human form. It would take Grant about six seconds to shift into his mountain lion.

Six seconds where he and Caitlyn would both be unprotected.

Worse, Mathers wasn't the only animal in the trees surrounding them.

There was no time for thinking it out. His shirt would rip on its own, but the jeans could hold him back. He tugged off his pants and shoes, then dropped to all fours and let out his lion. Bones lengthened, broke, and grew back together. His limbs lengthened and his skin itched like fire as fur sprouted all over his skin.

When the light around him faded, he looked up to see where Mathers was. Not coming toward Grant, like Grant had expected, but running after Caitlyn. Fuck.

He'd never reach Mathers in time to save Caitlyn.

Another grizzly barreled from the trees and collided with Mathers.

Hell yeah. Carter was here.

The two grizzlies fought, swiping at each other. Too late, Grant remembered that Mathers hadn't been the only enemy nearby. A wolf crashed into him, tearing a chunk out of his hide when he spun to swing the wolf away. Damien Buenevista. Buenevista was almost as bloodthirsty as Mathers, and he was a helluva good fighter. Grant had needed all his strength and wits the past two nights to keep Buenevista and Mathers from breaking past him and into the trailer where Caitlyn slept.

The grizzlies bellowed. Confident that Carter had Mathers covered, Grant twisted to dodge another blow from Buenevista, who fell to his side when he missed Grant. Growling, Grant swiped across the wolf's exposed chest with his claws.

A yowl was the only warning he had before a mountain lion collided with him. Fucking Derrick Alleman. Grant didn't need this. Two against him, and his hind leg was bleeding like a fuckin' fountain.

Time to go on the offensive. Before Buenevista could recover, Grant slashed his claws over his snout, sending a spray of blood outward. Just as much blood trickled over the wolf's eyes, temporarily blinding him. Then he rounded on Alleman, who was readying for another attack. While that genius puzzled out the best way to come at Grant, Grant charged.

Surprised, Alleman dodged, but the idiot lifted his

head and his neck was momentarily exposed. Grant went for it and bit down. Not hard enough for a kill, but hard enough to show he meant business.

One of these days, Alleman would die in one of these fights. But that day wasn't today, and Grant wasn't gonna be the beast to kill him.

Alleman kicked with his hind legs, trying to dislodge Grant, but it was no use. Grant bit down harder and harder. *Give up, asshole*, he thought.

Finally, Alleman went limp and closed his furious eyes, admitting defeat.

Well, at least the battle was out of the way. Mathers, Alleman, and Buenevista would leave him alone for another night.

Grant wondered if any of Mathers's other allies were in the woods, biding their time, but none of them came forward. He limped in the direction of his trailer, and Carter joined him along the way. He was limping, too, favoring one of his front legs.

When they reached Grant's trailer, they both shifted back into human. Carter groaned in pain as he stood up straight. Grant knew how he felt; his right thigh was mangled from where Buenevista had taken out a chunk.

Grant sniffed the air and smelled vanilla and roses—Caitlyn was around. Hopefully inside with the door locked. He knocked on the door and heard an answering gasp.

"It's me, Grant," he said, leaning his head against the wall of the trailer. "Carter and I are hurt."

She opened the door and took in their naked forms.

Her eyebrows shot up, but she didn't say anything about clothes. "Do you have bandages, antiseptic?"

"Nothing'll get infected," Grant said.

For a moment, she looked like she might argue.

"Your leg is bleeding," she finally said. "It's an open wound, and I'm wrapping it."

"We don't have first-aid kits here," Carter said, his voice a growl.

"Fine," she snapped. "I'll find a clean shirt. And what happened to you?"

"Something's out of place," he said. "Shifting didn't help."

Sometimes the process of shifting could help heal them, as their bodies found the alternate ways of putting themselves together. But sometimes it didn't work.

Caitlyn went inside the trailer and came back a moment later with two of Grant's white t-shirts. He wanted to protest about getting bloodstains on his clothes because it was so freaking hard to wash things here, but he took one look at the stern expression on her face and decided to keep his mouth shut.

She efficiently wrapped up his leg. Snug, but not too snug. Her gaze on his body was assessing and clinical, and he wanted to return to their moment earlier in the morning when her body had been pressed against his while they kissed.

"Do we need to worry about them coming back?" Caitlyn asked. "Shouldn't we, I don't know, fortify the trailer or something?"

"They won't bother us today," Carter said, his arm hanging awkwardly at his side.

"Okay. You're next," Caitlyn said, pointing at Carter.

He stepped forward, but then he growled when her hands came around his bicep.

"Watch it," Grant said to him.

"Looks like it's dislocated," Caitlyn said, feeling along the muscles and joints.

Carter breathed in and out. "No shit."

"Don't be rude," Caitlyn said. "Here."

She grabbed his wrist and guided the arm straight in front of Carter. He swore loudly until there was a loud cracking sound, and then he swore again. His face was pale, and sweat beaded along his brow. His blue eyes were dull with pain.

"You're all set," Caitlyn said.

"Thanks," Carter mumbled. He stood up and walked away, bare-ass naked.

Caitlyn turned her gaze on Grant.

"What?" he said, unable to read her expression.

"You turned into a cougar."

"Yep. I told you I could do that."

"And Carter was a bear."

Grant nodded. "Right again."

She leaned against the side of the trailer and closed her eyes. "It's a lot. Especially when you're standing there with your dick out."

"Yep." Laughing to himself, Grant went into the trailer and rummaged in the drawers beneath the bed. He found an old pair of sweatpants, pulled them on carefully over his wrapped leg, then went back out again.

So much had happened, and it wasn't even lunchtime yet.

Caitlyn was still leaning against the side of the trailer. Her head was resting against the belly of the mountain lion he'd painted onto the siding, and he inwardly preened at the sight. She'd chosen the lion.

She opened her eyes and stared at Grant when he came over to stand next to her.

"I don't know if it's any easier to have a conversation with you when you aren't wearing a shirt," she said.

"You want me to put one on?" he asked. The warm summer air felt nice against his skin, but he'd put on more clothes if that's what she really wanted.

"No...I'll get used to it."

He wanted her to get used to more than that. He wanted to show her more about himself, and find out if she'd go running away—or come running into his arms. He wanted another kiss with her luscious lips, a taste of that sweet tongue sliding against his.

But for now, he wanted to get to know her better.

"C'mon," he said, tugging on a pair of sneakers he'd left by the door. "Let's go for a walk."

"After those—those guys—just tried to kill us?" she asked, doubt all over her face. She didn't budge from the side of the trailer. He wondered if she viewed it as some kind of protected area, like the place kids would declare a safe zone if they reached it while playing tag.

"It's hard to explain," he said, "but basically, I established dominance for at least another day. The men don't follow many rules. Maybe they don't follow *any* rules. But their animal sides recognize dominance. And since I just handed them their asses—with Carter's help, but it still counts—we have some time to explore."

He held out his hand to her. *Please let her take it, please let her take it...*

She took it.

Smiling to himself, he started off, Caitlyn at his side.

"Where are we going?" she asked.

"I thought you might like to see the lake."

"Yeah, I'd love that," she said. "If nothing else, I can rinse off my stinky feet. I'd kill for a bath right now."

"I'll keep watch while you bathe," he offered.

She sent him a side-eye. "Really."

"Really." He held a hand over his heart. "I'll watch *away* from the lake, okay?"

It was only a ten-minute walk to the water.

"Tell me about your work," he said.

"Well, I'm a nurse. Which I told you."

He waited, then said, "You told me you *worked* in a hospital. Like in the past. Did you mean you don't anymore?"

"I quit to take care of my aunt. My mom passed away a few years ago, and I'm all my aunt had. She was wealthy, and a misanthrope. We'd never gotten along, and she hadn't gotten along with my mother, either—didn't even come to the funeral. Basically, when she found out her cancer was terminal, she told me that if I came to take care of her for the remainder of her time, she'd leave me everything she owned."

"Wow." He gave her hand a gentle squeeze.

Caitlyn nodded and squeezed his hand back. "The thing was, she didn't have to make me take care of her like that. Bribe me with her estate. I'd have done it anyway."

"I bet you would have."

She looked up at him, her brown eyes shining. "Thank you. Sometimes even I question my motivations. I wasn't happy down in L.A. Maybe I was using Aunt Galinda as an excuse to run away."

"Or," Grant said slowly, "maybe you needed her as much as she needed you?"

Caitlyn made a *hmm* sound and looked ahead of them. "I see it—the lake. Are we alone?"

He listened and sniffed the air. "Yep, we're alone."

"Great." She tugged off her shoes and the shirt she'd borrowed from him. "Well, stop gawking, creeper. I'm going to get clean and I don't need an audience."

"Okay, okay." He turned around, reluctantly, and listened to her finish undressing.

Then he listened to her rapid footsteps as she hurried to the water. She waded in and he heard her soft shriek.

"What is it?" he asked, starting to turn around.

"Nothing—don't look!"

He turned back around.

"It's just...it's colder than ice!"

He laughed. "Missing Los Angeles yet?"

"Ha. No, not really."

She splashed for a few more minutes, then went quiet.

"You okay?" Grant asked, keeping his eyes on the trees in front of him. But oh, how he wanted to look.

"Do you...do you want to come in?" she asked, her voice sounding shy.

Grant turned around in surprise. She stood in the

lake, water up to her navel, arms crossed over her chest. As he watched, she dropped her arms.

Fucking glorious.

"You look like some sort of water goddess," he said, kicking off his shoes and striding forward.

Her cheeks were pink with a blush, but she didn't hide herself from him. He yanked off his sweatpants, then waded toward her. The cold water was a mild shock at first, but he was used to it. Water soaked the t-shirts she'd tied around his thigh, but he didn't look down to see if the wound was healed or not. He didn't take his gaze from her as he closed the distance between them.

He gathered her in his arms, but stopped when his mouth was a few inches from hers. "Do you want this?" he asked.

"Want what, exactly?"

"Me. You. Screwing in a lake."

She laughed. "Yes, I want this."

"Good. Because I want it, too, in case you couldn't tell."

She pressed forward until her stomach was flush against his cock. "Yeah, I think I can tell."

He knew of a smooth, flat rock not far from the little beach, even more protected by a thick copse of trees surrounding it. He sometimes used it for drying his clothes after he washed them.

"Come here, you," he said, then lifted her from the water.

Laughing, she wrapped her legs around his waist. He bit back a curse that was half-dismay, half-victory. Her pussy was so close to his cock, all he'd have to do is lower her down a little bit and he'd be inside of her.

There was the rock. He walked out of the lake with her in his arms and set her on it. She shivered, and he kissed her mouth, closing his eyes in pleasure at how good she tasted, how much he wanted her.

"Couple things you should know," he said, pulling back. He'd just realized something tragic—birth control. It was a thing.

"Mmm, yeah?" She glanced up, her hands splayed on his chest.

"I have bad news. So, shifters don't carry diseases or get sick."

"That's good news, though," she said, looking at him in puzzlement.

"However," he said, "we can get human women pregnant. And I don't have a condom."

She tugged him closer. "It's okay. I have an IUD. If you're sure about the whole diseases thing..."

"Positive." He pressed a soft kiss to her lips. "I wouldn't do anything to hurt you. And if you aren't comfortable with this"—he took his cock in his hand and gave it a squeeze, loving the feeling but loving even more the way her eyes widened and she gave off a scent of fresh arousal—"there are different things we can do, too. I'm creative."

"I hope to see some of that," she said with a wink.

"Then allow me to demonstrate."

Standing in the lake before where she lay on the rock, he kissed his way up one of her legs. Goosebumps formed on her skin as he went. She moaned quietly. He approached her pussy and his kisses became open-mouthed so he could taste as much of her skin as possible. Past her knee. Up her thigh. And when he reached her center and placed an open-mouthed kiss there, he moved his tongue against her.

"Grant," she gasped.

"Mmm?" He didn't stop kissing, and he brought up a finger to press inside of her.

"Keep going," she said, wrapping her fingers in his hair. "Just like that."

Happy to oblige, he continued kissing and licking her, adding a second finger to her pussy and crooking them up a little. Caitlyn's moans grew louder, so he paused to listen for anyone nearby. They were still alone.

"I want to come," she said, looking down at him with her face flushed pink.

He gave himself a slow stroke and she licked her lips, her gaze on his length.

"Do you want to come on my mouth or my cock?" he asked. His dick ached with wanting her, but he'd let her finish however she chose.

"Cock."

Fuck yeah, he could do that. "Come here, lover."

He helped her forward a little bit, then leaned toward her. The head of his cock dragged against her thigh and came to rest next to her pussy. He bit back a swear word. So good. She felt so good in his arms. He couldn't shake the feeling that they belonged together like this. The thought had crossed his mind in the morning when they'd kissed, but now he was certain.

This woman was his mate.

Gripping his cock, he guided it to her entrance and slowly pushed inside. She tensed, so he waited.

"Is everything okay?" he asked.

"Yeah. You're just big. Go slow?"

"Got it." He pressed forward another little bit. A quarter inch? A half? He tried to focus on incremental measures of distance so he wouldn't lose control and blow his load before he was even half inside of her. She felt that good, her walls squeezing the head of his dick.

"More," she whispered.

After a few more stops and starts, he was all the way inside of her. She clutched his biceps, her nails digging slightly into his skin. When she lifted her hips and pulled back, he followed her lead, slowly fucking her with patient thrusts.

"Yes," she gasped. "Feels good. You?"

"You feel fucking amazing on my cock," he said. "I can't wait to feel you come."

Her breaths came faster and faster. He lowered his head to kiss her mouth. Keeping one hand on her hip, he brought his other up to caress one of her breasts. Her movements became more and more erratic, so he quickened his thrusts to match her unspoken urges.

She came with a shout, her pussy squeezing him rhythmically. He kissed her, drinking in her cries of pleasure, and stroked inside of her rapidly until he came, too. Electric pleasure shot through him and he fell next to her on the great rock, spent.

Curling on her side, Caitlyn snuggled next to him. He kissed her forehead and then they dozed in the warm afternoon.

8

Caitlyn held Grant's hand as they walked back to his trailer. It was dusk. The nap had been rejuvenating, the bath cleansing. The sex had been mind-blowing, and she wanted to do it again as soon as possible. It had been so long since she'd been with anyone, and her body wanted to make up for lost time.

It wasn't just the sex, though—it was Grant. There was something about him. Her body reacted to his in a way that she'd never experienced before. Chaos, heat, passion. There was a sense of wholeness that defied reason and explanation.

He felt *right*.

"You doing okay?" he asked.

"Yeah," she said. "Better than okay."

They'd reached his place. Her thoughts swirled in her head, much like the swirling colors of the painted animals on the camp trailer.

He noticed her staring at them and asked, "What do you think?"

"They're beautiful." She reached out to trace the snarling mouth of a leopard and shivered. "They look so alive. I mean, no animal really looks like this, exactly. They aren't realistic. But they carry...the spirit, I guess?"

"That's what I was going for."

"You painted these," she said, trying not to sound surprised.

He nodded and she detected a flash of pride in his expression.

"I probably sounded like an idiot trying to describe them," she added with a laugh.

"Not at all." He grabbed her hand and traced the panther's mouth with her, his fingers intertwined with hers.

She leaned back into his chest, allowing his warmth to envelop her.

"Is this what you do with your free time, usually?" she asked. "Paint?"

"Yep. I paint what I see in the shifters here. This leopard, that's a guy named Ronan. The bear over there—"

"Let me guess—Carter?" The bear wore an expression of fierce antagonism, yet his blue eyes were definitely Carter's, and they held an honesty within.

"Right in one," Grant said.

She noticed there wasn't another bear—Mathers didn't have a place on Grant's trailer. She was glad; she was just superstitious enough to believe that something like that would give her nightmares.

"I wish I'd found something creative to do with my time," Caitlyn murmured.

"When you were taking care of your aunt?"

"Mm-hmm. I had so much time alone, and I didn't know how to use it. She wanted a quiet house and she wanted me available to her all the time. My only break outside of the house was for my daily run."

"But you didn't have to sit next to her the whole time, did you?" Grant asked.

"No—she would've hated that," Caitlyn said. Poor Aunt Galinda. Lonely, but even in the end she had pushed Caitlyn away. "I spent most of my time in the house so I could hear her if she called for me. I read a lot of books, did a lot of baking. Now I wish I'd done something like painting."

"Maybe we could paint together sometime," Grant said.

She turned in his arms and looked into his kind, rugged face. "I'd like that."

He kissed her—softly, sweetly. When he pulled back, Caitlyn felt as if she'd gotten a hit of some kind of drug. It was a giant serotonin hit.

"Kiss me again," she said, and he did.

Maybe it was serotonin. Or maybe it was magic. What had he called it before? Fate?

Finally, they pulled apart, and Caitlyn said, "I think it's bedtime."

"I think so, too," he said, kissing her once more, a soft smack on the lips that made her crave another.

When he went inside the trailer, she hesitated. This nightmare situation—trapped in some kind of invisible dome with dangerous beast-men—had somehow turned into a fantasy. No, she wouldn't be happy, she couldn't rest, until she and Grant were free. But while they waited, they didn't have to be miserable.

She would only be miserable without him.

He was what she needed—his love, his companionship. Her aunt had died alone, and Caitlyn had decided she wanted more out of life than her career and casual friendships. Now she'd found what she needed. She'd found Grant.

Grinning to herself, she opened the trailer door to go inside.

Grant was coming out, and she collided against him.

"Careful, there," he said, grabbing her shoulders so she wouldn't fall.

"Where are you going?" she asked.

"I'll stay outside tonight, to guard you."

"Carter said they wouldn't come back tonight, didn't he?"

"Yeah. I think you'll be more comfortable and secure without me in there. I figured you'd want some space."

She touched his arm. "You figured wrong."

He stared directly into her eyes, his green irises captivating. "Why, Caitlyn Dorsey, are you inviting me to spend the night with you?"

"Yes—"

The word was hardly out of her mouth before he picked her up. Automatically, she wrapped her legs around his waist. He pressed her against the doorway and kissed her breathless. When he moved along her jaw and down to her neck, she gasped and clutched him more tightly against her.

More. She wanted more. Always, with him. Was there

a version of Stockholm Syndrome where two prisoners fell in love? Because she had no other explanation for the desperate feelings she had for this man. The need and desire had come out of nowhere.

They had to get out of this place—the Junkyard—so she could see if the feelings were just as strong outside of this fucked-up situation. Which reminded her...

"There's one thing we haven't talked about yet," she said, pulling back from his kisses.

"Yeah?"

"That white crystal that the...witch wants us to get?" She nearly tripped on the word *witch*. It still felt bizarre to talk about witches and shapeshifters as real people, not pretend Halloween caricatures. Would she get used to it, or would she forget all about this place after she was free?

She never wanted to forget Grant.

"It's not going to be easy to get it," Grant said. He ran his fingers through her hair, which sent delicious tingling feelings all through her body. "I know where to find white crystals—along the boundary, past the pond where we talked to Phillip yesterday. It's practically in Alleman's and Buenevista's back yards."

"But, if you're the dominant one, can't you go in and take it?"

"Not if it's their personal space. Unless I want to challenge them again. And it wouldn't be just those two fighting me, but everybody over there."

"So," she said, walking two fingers up his muscular pecs, over his neck, and up to his lips, "we're going to go in, all sneaky-like?"

"Close." He took the tips of her fingers in his teeth and gave them a gentle bite. As she shivered and felt her brain short-circuit with lust, he added, "*I'll* be going in, all sneaky-like, while you stay here where it's safe."

She thought of arguing with him, but she knew her strengths. She was not sneaky. A shifter could probably hear a mouse fart at three miles away, and Caitlyn couldn't compete with that.

"Are you worried about this?" she asked.

He grinned down at her. "Not at all."

"Good. When are you going to do it? Tonight?"

"Nope," he said. "Tomorrow night."

"Then let's go to bed."

"I like the way you think."

When she raised her mouth toward his, he pressed his lips to hers.

"Kissing you is like coming alive again," he whispered.

It was the same for her—like she'd been sleepwalking through her life up until now. But instead of pulling away to tell him about it, she showed him with her lips, her tongue, and the rest of her body.

9

"You'll stay here, fight with anyone who gets close," Grant said to Carter the following night. The woods were quiet, save for the occasional whoop of laughter coming from the dump, far-off. This late at night, way past midnight, most of the shifters were probably sleeping. All the easier for sneaking around.

Carter nodded and his blue eyes flashed. "Yes. Fuck. How many times are you going to tell me?"

Grant didn't trust Carter for much of anything, but he was Grant's only chance at a guard.

Caitlyn stood in the doorway of the trailer, looking nervously between them.

"Maybe you should shift to your bear now," Grant said, "so you're prepared if they come."

"I agreed to be a fucking babysitter." Carter plucked a long piece of grass from beside one of the wooden blocks holding up the trailer and stuck the end in his mouth. "I didn't agree to be bossed around by an overprotective mate."

Alarmed by Carter's use of the word *mate*, Grant flicked a glance at Caitlyn again. She mouthed the word with a question in her eyes, but Grant said, "Later."

He didn't know how he was going to bring that up to her. He was hers, forever. That was how it worked. But she was human. Did she feel the same things he felt?

He was hers, forever...but was she his?

Carter parked in the old lawn chair and leaned his head back against the side of the trailer, looking more like an old cowpoke with hay in his mouth than a brutal bodyguard.

"You're not inspiring my confidence," Grant growled.

Shrugging, Carter said, "You're not inspiring my desire to sit here and take your shit."

Caitlyn laughed. "Go, Grant. I'll be fine—I'll stay inside."

"This'll take me half an hour, tops," he said, marching forward and kissing her on the mouth.

"See you soon." Her eyes sparkled with playfulness, so he reached behind her and pinched her ass. She yelped and swatted his arm.

Carter made a fake retching sound.

"Okay, okay, I'm going," Grant said.

He planted one last kiss on Caitlyn's nose, ignoring the gagging noises coming from Carter, then jogged west through the woods that would lead him past Carter's place and all the way across the Junkyard to the dump, where Mathers and a few of the others had created their dens.

When he got closer to the dump, he slowed his pace and kept to the shadows. The moon was just a sliver in the sky. Grant inhaled, exhaled. He watched the edges of the dump, where old trucks and cars had been piled together in a grotesque, rusting kind of fence. He didn't see anyone patrolling, but really, why would Mathers put anybody up to that? The only guys who lived outside of the dump were Grant and Carter. As far as Mathers and the rest of them thought, Grant and Carter had no reason to come here.

Grant darted forward and paused next to a rusting school bus. The stale beer stink of Derrick Alleman was all over the place, and it was fresh, but Alleman was nowhere in sight. Grant edged around the bus and ran to a pile of sheet metal leaning against some other junk.

The sound of heavy mouth-breathing was the only warning he had. Ducking, he dodged the blow to his neck. The jagged ends of a broken bottle caught him in the shoulder instead.

"The fuck?" he hissed.

Derrick Alleman stood in front of him, a sneer on his face. "Why are you sneaking around our territory?"

"Just going for a walk," Grant said, before swiping against Alleman's ankles with his foot and taking him down. He clocked Alleman hard in the face and nodded in satisfaction as Alleman's eyes closed.

"You give mountain lion shifters a bad name," Grant added.

His shoulder hurt like hell and he was probably bleeding everywhere, but he wanted to get that crystal and get the fuck out of here.

He passed the giant pile of wood and metal that was Stetson's den before he came to another ring of rusted vehicles. Alleman and Buenevista lived somewhere in here. Jase, too, if Grant wasn't mistaking the scent of sandalwood.

Behind Alleman's and Buenevista's places was a pile of rubble dotted with clear and white crystals. Grant had seen it once or twice when combing through the dump for cans of paint. On those trips, he'd been here with permission. Now, they'd just as soon as kill him as look at him, as Alleman had demonstrated with that broken bottle.

He heard talking nearby, but the dump was strangely quiet, and that bothered him more than anything else. Hurrying forward, he snatched a shining crystal from the pile of rubble and retraced his steps. The sooner he could get back to Caitlyn and send Carter on his not-so-merry way, the better. He jammed the stupid rock in his pocket for safekeeping.

On his way out, he passed Alleman next to the bus. Kicking the asshole was a temptation, but Grant restrained himself and kept moving. Once he was back in the woods, he relaxed out of stealth mode and moved faster, no longer concerned with discovery.

Something niggled at his mind as he hurried to the trailer. A feeling of urgency. He let it propel him forward even faster until he was running.

There was his trailer. He came around to the front of it. Carter was nowhere in sight.

"Carter," he said.

Had he abandoned his post?

"Caitlyn?" Grant yanked open the door and went

inside. Her vanilla rose scent met his nostrils, but it was tinged with the acrid scent of her fear.

And the sour scent Mathers carried.

"Caitlyn!" Fuck. Fuck. Where could she be?

It had been quiet at the dump—while he was going there, had they all been coming here?

No time to waste. He followed Carter's and Caitlyn's scents. They mingled with Mathers's sour scent, and then Caitlyn's vanilla got fainter. She'd been carried.

Mathers had touched her. Held her. Carried her away. She must have been terrified. Choking through his own fear, terrified that Caitlyn was hurt and scared, Grant ran forward.

Loud shouting reached his ears. He abandoned the scent trail and followed the noise. It took him toward Carter's place, which was smack in the middle of the Junkyard.

He heard a grunt of pain, and Carter mumbled, "Sonuvabitch."

Grant rushed through the trees until he could see Carter's ramshackle den, which was made mostly of fallen logs and rusted sheet metal. Next to it was a small clearing. Two lanterns rested on the ground, illuminating the scene, but one had been kicked on its side. Good thing they were electric lanterns—no forest fires today.

Caitlyn was nowhere in sight, but Carter was shirtless and facing a shirtless opponent—Noah Ephraimson, a blond-haired wolf shifter with a long Viking beard. Another guy stood nearby, blood trickling from a cut on his eyebrow.

Noah growled at Carter. He pulled back an arm, but

Grant jumped forward and grabbed him before he could swing.

"Where—is—she?" Grant demanded, throwing Noah to the ground and holding a foot over his throat.

"Fuck, what the hell, man?" Carter said, pulling Grant away from Noah.

Noah got up, growling. He looked like he was ready to tear off his jeans and shift into his wolf.

"I got this," Carter said.

Grant stared hard at Carter. "You weren't fighting him to get Caitlyn?"

Carter threw back his head and laughed. "Why would I do that? She's at the trailer." Then understanding seemed to hit him. "Oh shit. She's not at the trailer."

"No," Grant growled.

"Bummer."

Grant didn't think. He hauled an arm back and swung. His fist caught Carter in the chin.

"What the fuck?" Carter said.

"Where is she?"

"I don't know." Carter rubbed his jaw.

"Why'd you leave?"

"Why do I do anything?" Carter asked. "My bear wanted a fight. I rustled up a couple of guys so I could give him one."

Grant shook his head. "You're disgusting."

"Try the south end of the dump," Carter said, spitting blood on the ground. "Mathers probably took her there."

Grant started off, cursing under his breath.

"For what it's worth," Carter called after him, "I hope you get her back."

It was worth nothing, coming from the mouth of a guy who couldn't keep his fucking beast in control long enough to guard Grant's mate. But Grant didn't have time to fight with him.

He had a whole different battle ahead of him.

10

Stars studded the night sky, and a crescent moon hung near the eastern horizon. It wasn't dawn yet, and Caitlyn guessed there was maybe an hour to go before the witch could meet them. She gritted her teeth at the feeling of the rough rope binding her hands. She was in a cage with rusted metal bars. Other than that, she had no idea where she was. It had been dark before, when she'd been in Mathers's trailer, but nothing around here looked familiar. She couldn't see the thick gravel line that showed where the edge of the Junkyard was. How big was this place? Mathers had said something like it was less than a hundred acres.

That meant Grant would be able to find her. She just had to trust him.

A few men, four including Mathers, leaned against an old Mustang. It was a crime what had happened to that car—rust and years of neglect had turned it into a pocked relic from another era. And now people like Mathers were resting their ugly asses against it.

The men passed a bottle back and forth, drinking clear liquid from it. From the way they laughed and got louder and louder, Caitlyn would've bet her favorite pair of scrubs that they weren't drinking water.

Mathers caught her looking at him and smiled. She glared harder, until he reached down and cupped his junk through his jeans.

Disgusting. She looked away, and he cackled.

"I think our prize is getting impatient," Mathers said to the others.

"I know I sure as hell am," one of them said.

"Just like last time," Mathers said. "Last man standing takes her, claims her, and she's yours."

"You sure Lewiston isn't hiding somewhere, ready to steal her away?"

"Let him try," Mathers said with a growl.

Yeah, let him try, Caitlyn thought. He'd be here, no question. It should've only taken him a half hour to get that crystal, and by now he would know she was missing.

Why hadn't Carter done anything? Caitlyn had been sitting in the trailer, wondering what to do with her time while she waited for Grant to come back. The next thing she knew, Mathers had yanked open the door and came inside. He'd half-dragged, half-carried her here, where all those other goons had been waiting.

"You're weak," he'd said, his sour breath in her face. "And soon, you'll be mine."

She'd been too terrified to cuss him out. Anger and fear still had a hold on her. But every time the emotions got to be too much, she'd think of Grant. He'd be here any second.

While Mathers and the other guys argued over who would fight first, Caitlyn took a more careful look at her cage. The bars were old and a couple of them looked fragile near the bottom. Carefully, Caitlyn inched sideways. Maybe she could rub the rope against one of the sharp edges, or kick the bar out entirely.

When Mathers looked her way again, she slumped down to the metal floor of the cage and leaned against the rustiest bars. Let her seem fragile to him. Let her seem "weak," like he'd said. Fuck him and his supposed strength. You couldn't prove you were strong by bullying others.

He immediately went back to organizing the first match, between him and one of the others. Caitlyn pushed and pulled on the bar directly behind her and felt a slight give.

She just might have a chance.

Mathers threw the first punch, and Caitlyn timed a big shove against the bar to happen while the others were calling out encouragements. It seemed they wanted the other guy to win so they could fight him instead of Mathers.

The bar came loose, leaving a jagged edge. She began working the rope back and forth. While the guys fought, her arms grew sore. This wasn't a motion she was used to making. Still, she wasn't weak. She was going to keep doing this until she was free.

"Caitlyn, don't turn around."

It was Grant's voice, coming from the shadows behind her. She almost cried with relief.

"I need to know if they're looking this way," he whispered. "Don't say anything, just lift up one of your fingers if it's safe for me to come over there and rip another bar from the cage."

Her heart thumped wildly in her chest. She couldn't let Grant get caught by the others.

The other guy growled and leaped at Mathers. All of them were distracted by the fight. She lifted her pinky and felt the cage jerk as one of the bars was ripped away.

Grant's hands came over her upper arms and he helped lift her up, then guided her out of the cage. A second later, he tore away the rope binding her wrists.

"How did you do that?" she whispered.

"You got the break in the rope started," he said, leaning into her and pressing his face into her hair. "Fuck, I was so scared for you. Here." Grant pressed something warm and hard into her hand. The crystal. "Take this and go to the witch."

"Not without you," Caitlyn said.

He turned intense green eyes on her and shook his head. "If I can get there, I will. But you need to get out, Caitlyn. You're more important than anything else I do here. Please. Go. I don't want you to be late."

Tears filled her eyes. She didn't want to leave without him. Her heart felt like it was cracking open at the very idea.

"Please—"

"The *fuck*?" a loud voice called from the group of fighters.

"Go," Grant said, pointing.

Caitlyn ran.

The sharp edges of the crystal dug into her palm, she held it so tightly.

Beastly roars rose up behind her, filling her ears. Was Grant turning into a cougar? Would he be safe? Her legs pumped faster, and she kept moving in the direction Grant had indicated.

The sky lightened—the sun was rising. The witch had said dawn. Shit. Would Caitlyn make it in time? How long would the witch wait?

Then she slowed. An old delivery truck lay on its side and she leaned against it, breathing hard. As strange as everything was that had happened here in the past few days, Caitlyn loved Grant. That was the strangest of all. She *loved* him and she'd only just met him.

And she would fight for him. She wouldn't give up, hide from love like her aunt had done. She would go after it with a...with a... She looked around until she spotted a giant metal pipe. Tucking the crystal into her sports bra, she grabbed the pipe and hoisted it in her hand.

She'd fight for Grant, for love, and for their future—whether that future would take place here in the Junkyard or out there in the free world.

She ran again—this time not away from trouble, but toward it.

When she reached Grant and the others, she found them in the midst of a heated battle. Four against one, Grant in the center of it.

One of the men spotted her and left the fight, rushing toward her. She held the pipe in her arms, praying her adrenaline would give her the strength she needed.

They thought she was weak. She'd use that. She pretended to struggle with the weight of the pipe.

The guy smiled. "Is that too heavy for you, sweetheart?"

"No?" She pretended to tremble.

He reached forward, still smiling.

Giving him a smile of her own, she lifted and swung the pipe at the same time. It caught him beneath the chin. He didn't go down, but he fell back with a curse. His movement distracted Mathers, and Grant took the opportunity to give Mathers a roundhouse kick to the throat.

Mathers fell down, choking, and the other guys paused.

"You can try to win this," Grant said, "but you're gonna lose."

Mathers rolled on the ground, clutching his neck.

"So?" Grant said.

None of the guys stepped forward.

Satisfied, Grant nodded and walked over to Caitlyn. "You okay?"

"I'm good," she said. "Is Mathers going to die?"

Grant gave him a scornful look. "Sadly, no." He held out an arm to her. "Shall we?"

Caitlyn nodded and linked her arm with his. Together, they walked to the edge of the Junkyard where the witch was supposed to meet them.

"Do you think we'll make it in time?" Caitlyn asked.

"I hope so."

A few minutes later, they passed the small pond. Caitlyn could make out the shape of a person in the distance.

"It's her," Caitlyn said. "I think she's turning around."

She and Grant dropped each other's arms and ran.

"Wait for us!" Caitlyn shouted. "We're coming!"

The figure paused. Caitlyn and Grant kept running until they skidded to a stop at the line of gravel. The witch faced them, her pale blond hair nearly white and falling in a straight sheet down her back. Her eyes were so dark, they were nearly black.

Caitlyn bent at the waist, trying to catch her breath. Looking up from her bent position, she gasped, "I'm Caitlyn, and this is Grant."

"I'm Maddie," the woman said.

"Hi, Maddie." Grant's deep voice resonated with hope. "Can you let us out of here?"

"You have the crystal?" Maddie asked.

Caitlyn fished the crystal out of her sports bra and showed it to her.

"Good. I'll let you out, but not him. I don't know him or why he's in there."

That wasn't the deal, was it?

"No," Caitlyn said. "You have to let both of us out of here. He's a good person. I...I love him."

"It's okay," Grant said. "It's more important that you get out."

Maddie eyed them curiously. "Are you mates?"

Mates? Carter had said something about that, but Caitlyn didn't know what it meant. "Like, how animals get together?" she asked.

"For life," Grant said, nodding. "Yes, we are. At least, I'm hers forever."

Tears filled Caitlyn's eyes as she looked into Grant's

determined face. "And I'm yours. I'm not leaving without you."

Cocking her head, Maddie looked at them again. "If you're mates, you can get out. Hold hands and come over."

"Really?" Caitlyn asked. It couldn't be that easy.

"The boundary will recognize your full hearts," Maddie said.

Caitlyn looked up at Grant. That was exactly what she felt when she was with him—a full, complete, whole heart. "Should we try this?"

11

Grant held Caitlyn's hand in his and looked down at her. He'd never loved anyone more than he loved her. He'd never wanted anything as much as he wanted her happiness and affection.

Maddie stared impassively at them from the other side of the gravel line with her creepy-as-night black eyes. "Well?"

This was it. The moment they would walk across the boundary and be free. Together.

He hated to hope for this, because he was afraid of being disappointed. What if it didn't work? What if they were both mistaken and they weren't mates? No, he knew without a doubt that they belonged together as mates—there was no question. But the witch could be wrong about the boundary's rules.

He tried to ignore the doubt and fear and focus on the hope instead. He looked at his mate and felt the fear dissipate.

"You ready?" he said to Caitlyn.

She nodded, and, looking into each other's eyes, they stepped over the gravel at the same time.

Grant sighed. Free. They were out at last, and they were together. Pulling Caitlyn into his arms, he gave her their first kiss as free people, outside of the Junkyard, ready to start a wonderful new life together. Caitlyn tasted like vanilla and she smelled sweet and rich like roses. He could kiss her all damn day, but there'd be time for that soon.

Keeping his arms around Caitlyn, Grant looked to Maddie. "Thank you."

Caitlyn handed Maddie the crystal.

"I didn't do anything," Maddie said, peering at the crystal. "But thanks for this. It will help with my spells."

She turned to go, but Caitlyn said, "Wait."

Maddie paused. "Yes?"

"There's another guy in there," Caitlyn said. "I don't think he belongs. His heart is good."

"You're not talking about Carter, are you?" Grant said, looking at her in surprise.

Her brown eyes were earnest. "I know he's done some bad things. But he's not a bad guy."

"I'm risking the alphas' wrath just talking to you two," Maddie said. "They don't want everyone to know how to get out of the Junkyard. If you want to tell your buddy, fine, but that's it."

With that, Maddie walked away, maybe so Grant and Caitlyn wouldn't be able to ask her any more questions.

Grant squeezed Caitlyn's hand, then moved his arm around her waist. "Carter, really?"

"Really." She tilted her head back, looking into Grant's eyes. She was tired, he could tell. It had been a long-ass night. But there was still a smile on her face. She stood on tiptoes and he bent forward slightly so she could kiss him. "He's a jackass, but he isn't all bad."

"The man can't stop with the violence," Grant said.

"Agree to disagree."

"Or you could just agree with me," he said.

She gave him a light smack on the shoulder. Grinning, he reached down and literally swept her off her feet, hauling her into his arms like she was his bride.

Hmm, *bride*. Not a bad idea. Yeah, he would marry her if she'd have him. But first he wanted to show her his place.

He carried her around the edge of the Junkyard, this time on the *outside* of that gravel line. The air was the same here. The trees looked and smelled the same. The forest noises were the same. Yet it felt different because they were free.

His cabin came into view, with the hammock on the front porch. He couldn't wait to show Caitlyn inside, and he hoped she would make the place her own.

He stepped up onto the porch and set Caitlyn down. "Wanna check it out?"

"Yeah, I do," she said.

He opened the door and they walked in. It was dusty and the food in the refrigerator was going to reek as soon as he pulled it open. He'd leave it closed, for now. The trash, thankfully, didn't stink—he'd taken it out shortly before he'd gone into the Junkyard.

He tried to see the cabin through Caitlyn's eyes, and

watched as she took in the homey-looking furniture—a simple couch, an easy chair facing the wood stove. No television. The bedroom was the same as the living room except with a bed and nightstand. Everything was simple, except the walls were covered in murals.

"This is amazing," she said, spinning around to take in the murals, her brown eyes wide in admiration. "I love it, Grant."

"Do you think you could live out here in the middle of nowhere with a Junkyard shifter like me?" he asked her.

Wrapping her arms around his neck, she said, "Yes. I'll choose you, and love, every time."

"Caitlyn Dorsey, I love you," he said. "I'm so happy you're my mate and my forever love."

"I love you, too, Grant Lewiston." She kissed his lips as he held her close, breathing in her scents of vanilla, roses, and happiness.

Loving the Junkyard Shifters? Find the next book, *Filthy Beast*, at your favorite retailer by visiting https://lizastreetauthor.com/lizas-books/junkyard-shifters or https://books2read.com/filthy-beast.

From *Filthy Beast*:

He hooked two fingers into her belt loop and dragged her closer. "How about you use that tongue for something good and kiss me?"

"Fuck you."

"Anytime, kitty cat."

The look she gave him was pure revulsion, but he

could scent her desire in the air. She might not like him right now, but she wanted him.

He could work with that.

"You think I'm the same as the other guys here?" he asked. "A violent fighter, ready to kick the shit out of anything that moves?"

"I know you are. I saw you in the ring," she said, her blue eyes revealing some of the hurt she felt.

"That wasn't me, kitty cat. That was the beast inside, trying to protect you."

"I don't need protecting."

He laughed and held up his forearm. The scratches she'd left there while in her cougar form still stung even though they were already starting to heal. "I know that, now."

"Sorry I hurt you," she said, looking down.

"Sorry I dragged you away from your fight. Now come here." He kept his fingers in her belt loop and wrapped his other arm around her waist. Her skin was so warm, he felt it through her shirt. "I want that kiss."

Get your copy at https://books2read.com/filthy-beast!

ALSO BY LIZA STREET

Fierce Mates: Sierra Pride

The Sierra Pride: The Complete Series

Fierce Wanderer

Fierce Heartbreaker

Fierce Protector

Fierce Player

Fierce Dancer

Fierce Informer

Fierce Survivor

Fierce Lover

Fierce Mates: Corona Pride

The Corona Pride: Books 1-5

Savage Yearning

Savage Loss

Savage Heartache

Savage Thirst

Savage Bliss

Savage Redemption

Irredeemable (a FREE prequel)

Savage Penance

Fierce Mates: Dark Pines Pride

The Dark Pines Pride: Books 1-3

Wild Homecoming

Wild Atonement

Wild Reunion

Wild Engagement

Fierce Mates: Rock Creek Clan

The Rose King

Ruthless Misfit

Ruthless Outlaw

Ruthless Fighter

Ruthless Rogue

Ruthless Knight

Junkyard Shifters

Filthy Vandal

Filthy Beast

Filthy Wolf

Filthy Alpha

Charmslinger

Blood Bounty

Blood Beast

Spellbound Shifters: Dragons Entwined

(with Keira Blackwood)

Dragons Entwined: Books 1-3

Dragon Forgotten (a FREE prequel)

Dragon Shattered

Dragon Unbroken

Dragon Reborn

Dragon Ever After

Spellbound Shifters: Fates and Visions

(with Keira Blackwood)

Oracle Defiant

Oracle Adored

Spellcaster Hidden

Spellbound Shifters Standalones

(with Keira Blackwood)

Hope Reclaimed

Orphan Entangled

Alphas & Alchemy: Fierce Mates

(with Keira Blackwood)

Claimed in Forbidden

Fated in Forbidden

Bound to Forbidden

Caught in Forbidden

Mated in Forbidden

Forever in Forbidden

Destined in Forbidden

ABOUT LIZA

Liza Street got her start in romance by sneak-reading her grandma's paperbacks. Now she's a *USA Today* bestselling author. Whether writing paranormal romance or urban fantasy, she delights in throwing humans and supernaturals together and watching the magical mayhem.

Join Liza's mailing list to get all the good news when it happens! Click here to visit https://lizastreetauthor.com/free-book/

CPSIA information can be obtained
at www.ICGtesting.com
Printed in the USA
LVHW010600020920
664633LV00006B/818